DUE

APR 0 8 1992		
4/19/94		
4/22/94		
4/25/94		

Making Up Your Mind About

DRUGS

GILDA BERGER

illustrated by Ted Enik

LODESTAR BOOKS   E. P. DUTTON   NEW YORK

Library of Congress Cataloging-in-Publication Data

Berger, Gilda.
  Making up your mind about drugs.

  "Lodestar books."
  Bibliography: p.
  1. Children—drug use—Juvenile literature.
2. Drug abuse—Prevention—Juvenile literature.
I. Enik, Ted. II. Title.
HV5824.C45B47 1988 362.2'93'088054 88-3609
ISBN 0-525-67256-7

Published in the United States by E. P. Dutton,
2 Park Avenue, New York, N.Y. 10016,
a division of NAL Penguin Inc.

Published simultaneously in Canada by
Fitzhenry & Whiteside Limited, Toronto

Editor: Virginia Buckley

Printed in the U.S.A.   COBE   First Edition
10 9 8 7 6 5 4 3 2 1

for Kenneth, with love

Acknowledgments

I would like to thank the following people for their help and encouragement: Bob Bakst and Barbara Sarah, Great Neck Public Schools, Great Neck, New York; Ron Saverese; and Carol Kroll, Nassau School Library System, Westbury, New York.

Contents

1   What Do You Do?   1

2   How Well Do You Know Yourself?   4

3   What Do You Know About Drugs?   15

4   Why Do Some Kids Say Yes to Drugs?   31

5   Why Is One Time Too Many?   44

6   How Can You Say No to a Friend?   56

7   How Can You Say No
      After You've Said Yes?   73

    Understand Some Terms   87

    Further Reading   89

.1.
What Do You Do?

You go to the movies with a friend. After the movie your friend's older brother offers to drive you home in his car. He has an open can of beer in his hand. Two empty cans are on the floor. He offers you a sip of beer. What do you do?

Your class is going on a weekend camping trip. Two friends tell you that they will be taking cigarettes along. They want you to do the same. You know that smoking is not allowed. What do you do?

You are at a wedding with your family. The adults are drinking a vodka punch. Your uncle offers you a sip of his drink. You are thirsty and would like to taste the punch. What do you do?

You go into the rest room at the shopping mall. Three kids from your school are there. They are passing around a marijuana cigarette and offer you a puff. What do you do?

A friend invites you to her party. She tells you that someone will be bringing wine. You've never had alcohol before, and you'd rather not start now. If you don't go, you're afraid that she won't ever invite you again.

If you do go, but don't drink, you're afraid your friends will make fun of you. What do you do?

Sooner or later, no matter where you live or how old you are, someone is going to offer you a drug. The drug could be a cigarette, a can of beer, or a marijuana joint. It might be a sniff of glue or a pill of some sort. Or it may be crack or another kind of drug.

Of course, whether or not you say no to drugs is up to you. But it helps to be informed. And to be informed, you should:

- know about yourself.
- know about drugs.
- know how to make wise decisions.

.2.
How Well Do You Know Yourself?

Like everyone else, you have your own ways of looking at things. You have your own opinions. You have your own ways of feeling and acting. And especially, you have your own ideas about who you are.

What you think of yourself is called your self-image or self-concept. People with a good self-concept are usually up on themselves. They see themselves as worthwhile and wonderful. Those with a poor self-concept are usually down on themselves. They feel that they are useless and second-rate.

Experts have discovered something special about kids who stay away from drugs. They are the same in a very important way. They like themselves. They have a good sense of who they are. And they're able to think for themselves. In other words, they have a good self-image.

The Way You See Yourself

Before we talk about your self-concept, there are two people we'd like you to meet.

Meet Jenny. She is someone who has a good self-image. She likes herself. Jenny sees herself as popular

and the leader in her group of friends. She can take criticism without going to pieces. When she feels strongly about something, she holds to her point of view, even if it makes other people angry. She is not afraid to stand up to parents or teachers when she believes that they are in the wrong.

Jenny is confident. She believes that she can solve most problems that come along. Because she has faith in her ability, things usually turn out well for her. Her success makes her feel good about herself. And her good feelings about herself make it easy for her to admire and respect others. They, in turn, enjoy being with her.

Now meet Peter. Peter has a poor self-image. He does not feel good about himself. He runs into difficulties wherever he turns. Convinced that he cannot succeed, he does not try very hard. "I can never do anything to please my parents, my teachers, or anybody else," he says. "Why should I even try? I'll just do what I want to do."

Peter's lack of effort usually leads to more failure. This brings down his confidence in himself. Because he usually goes along with what other people want, his friends call him wishy-washy. Most of the time he doesn't even know how to have fun. He has trouble making and keeping friends. All this drives his opinion of himself even lower.

People like Peter are often the ones who turn to drugs. Those like Jenny are less likely to experiment with drugs.

Here's a way to learn more about your own self-image. Take two sheets of paper. Make a list on one under the heading: "I like myself because . . ." Write down all the things about yourself that please you. Include character (honest, fair), personality (friendly, cheerful), abilities (athletic, musical), and anything else (animal lover, never lose temper) that you feel good about.

On the other paper list the things that you don't especially like about yourself. Do you occasionally lie? Are you shy and timid? Often angry? Do you sometimes bully smaller kids? Is it hard for you to make friends? Do you dislike people whose skin color or religion is different from yours?

Look over your lists. Check the many positive qualities. Note the various signs of strength and confidence. Then consider the negative qualities—the things that make you feel weak, powerless, or unsure of yourself.

All of us can make similar lists of things we like or don't like about ourselves. But did you ever stop to think that you can change some of your bad feelings about yourself? That you can take steps to improve your self-image—even if you're happy with the person you are?

Some experts suggest these ways to get a better self-concept:

1. Feel that you are loved by the important people in your life.

2. Believe that you are good at doing things that you consider important.

3. Take charge of your life and try to influence the lives of others.

No one says that reaching these goals is easy. Only that they are part of a good self-concept and that it's in your power to feel good about yourself.

How Others See You

The poet Robert Burns once wished that we could "see ourselves as others see us." But, in fact, we do. Our sense of who we are comes from what people tell us about ourselves.

Think for a moment about how you strike other people. Do they see you as quiet or loud? As shy or outgoing? Do they think of you as kind or selfish? Do they believe that you are athletic or clumsy? Smart or slow? That you have a great sense of humor or none at all?

Perhaps they think of you as being crazy about dancing. Or animals. Or cars. Or fixing things. They might admire your talent in drawing. Or playing the piano. Or working a computer.

How do you think the opinions of others compare with what you think of yourself? How do your friends' opinions differ from the opinions of family members?

Here's something interesting to try out. The results may tell you a lot about yourself.

1. Have a good friend write a short description of the kind of person you are.

2. Then have a close relative do the same.

3. Finally, write down a description of the kind of person you think you are.

Compare the three descriptions. Do they sound like the same person? Or are they all different? What do you think this means? Based on the results, would you say you see yourself as others see you?

What we think of ourselves and what our family thinks of us are often quite similar. For a very good reason. Our first ideas about the kind of people we are come from the people we live with.

For example, your parents say you are very stubborn. You don't really think so. But they say it so many times over so many years that you begin to think they may be right. They must know what they're talking about.

Gradually you start to think of yourself as hard-

headed. You get more and more fixed in your ways and your opinions. You refuse to change your mind about anything. You indeed act stubborn.

Research shows that children who are always told by their parents that they are stubborn—or clumsy, or stupid, or fat—grow up believing that they are. Often they live up to the idea, or image, that their mothers or fathers have of them. They become the kind of people the adults expect them to become.

Later, friends shape the opinions we have of ourselves. We care very much what they think of us. The more they admire and respect us, the better is our self-image.

The people we go to school with—our peers—help us decide who we are. They help us to discover our special ways of feeling, thinking, and acting. Many of our values and beliefs come from our friends.

From our peers we learn how to get along in the world. We come to know what is okay to do and what is not. From them we learn which things are important in life—when to hold out for what we want and when to give in.

Everyone is influenced by friends. Peer pressure is great on us all. Yet some kids go along with the crowd and get involved with drugs, and some do not. No one knows exactly why. But one thing is quite sure. The reason has to do with the opinion young people have of themselves.

How You Handle Your Feelings

We all have feelings. Good feelings—joy, happiness, satisfaction. And bad feelings—fear, anger, sadness.

The fact is, you couldn't live without your feelings. All of them! Feelings are a natural and necessary part of life. In the words of the writer Kahlil Gibran, feelings "are the rudder and sails of your seafaring soul." It's feelings that make you feel alive. And it's feelings that put energy and color into your life.

Not everyone, though, knows what to do with the feelings that he or she has. Especially the bad feelings.

For example, you and your two best friends are walking home from school. Someone from your class comes over and invites you all to a costume party.

One friend is not a very good dancer. He's afraid he may have to dance at the party. Still he agrees to go. "Between now and then," he says, "I'll learn some steps so I don't make a fool of myself. And even if I look clumsy—so what?"

Your other friend, though, turns down the invitation. He lies and says he can't make it. The reason is, he doesn't want to wear a costume. He's sure that he'll feel silly and that the others will make fun of him.

Both of your friends are feeling afraid. But one decides to face the thing that is making him fearful. The other decides to run away from the situation.

All of us need to learn how to handle the bad feelings we have. We must realize that everyone feels frightened or out of place sometimes. And we should know that there are always problems to work through.

What's important and helpful is to face up to the problems. We must try to do something about the bad feelings that are part of everyone's life. Some people do it very well. Others find it more difficult.

One of the best ways to handle feelings is to talk to

others. This can help you understand and get in touch with what is bothering you. It is also one of the quickest ways to get rid of bad feelings.

In the movies and on television, people always seem to say exactly what they feel. But in real life, it's much harder. Sometimes your feelings make you do or say things you might regret later on.

For example, your kid sister is always in your room touching your things. Once you see her taking your tapes out of their boxes and getting them all mixed up. You explode. "You're a little pest! I hate you! I feel like killing you!"

Your sister cries, and your parents punish you. Because of what happens when you express your feelings, you learn to bottle them up. But feelings that you bury will not stay locked up forever. They build inside you. You might develop headaches or get attacks of the blahs. Or you might look for a way to change how you feel.

For some people, changing how they feel means *doing* something to solve the problem. It can be talking things over with a parent, teacher, or friend. Or sitting alone and thinking through the situation. Getting busy is another solution. Some kids will decide to go for a long bike ride, bake a batch of cookies, sort their stamps or coins, work out in the gym, or something similar.

But for other people, handling feelings means *taking* something—a drink or a drug. The drug doesn't help them solve the problem. All it does is help them to forget that the problem exists. Then, when the effect of

the drug wears off, they've got a double problem: the original difficulty plus the troubles that the drug brings.

Growing up can be hard. So running away from a problem may sometimes seem like the best thing to do. But it never is. Drugs are a form of running away, or escape. Basically, they're unhealthy ways of dealing with bad feelings.

How about you? When you're feeling terrible, what do you do? Do you tend to *do* something? Or to *take* something?

Think of the last time you had a problem. Perhaps you were being forced to do something under pressure. Maybe you did something you were sorry you did. Or you had to make a tough decision.

What did you do? Were the results good? Could you have worked things out better?

Each person has to find the way that works best for him or her. But it helps to know that:

- bad feelings are signs of problems.
- problems are a normal part of everyday life.
- you can deal with problems if you face up to them.

People who get in the habit of solving small everyday problems are better able to handle big problems when they come along. Those who get used to running away from problems never learn how to work their way out of difficult situations.

Knowing how you see yourself and how others see you won't make all your problems go away. But it will surely help you handle them better.

.3.

What Do You Know About Drugs?

Growing up in America today, you can't help learning about drugs. You read about them in books, magazines, and newspapers. You see movies or television shows about drugs. And you hear about people who are hooked on them.

Your teachers may talk about drugs in school. You may see drugs being bought or sold on the streets. And you probably know at least one person who is smoking, drinking, or using some drug.

Sometimes, though, along with all this information on drugs come confusion and mistaken ideas. Perhaps now is a good time to get some things straight.

What Drugs Are

Drugs are chemicals. They are chemicals that change the way your mind and body work.

People take drugs when they are sick. These kinds of drugs are called medicines. They can be bought at any drugstore. An aspirin, for example, gets rid of the pain of a headache. Antibiotics kill the germs that cause a sore throat or fever.

But some drugs are not medicines. These are the

drugs that change the way you feel, think, and behave. Such drugs are called mind drugs.

Most mind drugs are illegal, or illicit. It is against the law for anyone to use them. Only a few, like alcohol or tobacco, are legal for people over a certain age.

The majority of illicit drugs cannot be bought in the drugstore. They are usually bought on the street from drug dealers, or pushers. Some mind drugs, such as sleeping pills, are sold in drugstores. But they are not intended for use as mind drugs. And substances such as glue and gasoline are sometimes misused as drugs. They can also be bought in stores.

These different kinds of mind drugs—legal and illegal—are what we are talking about in this book. The list is very long. It includes alcohol, tobacco, marijuana, heroin, cocaine, barbiturates, LSD, PCP, and the vapors of glue and gasoline.

We'll start with alcohol and tobacco. They are so common that people sometimes forget that they really are mind drugs.

Alcohol

Did you know that drinking alcohol is the number one drug problem of kids in America? More than half of sixth graders and more than one third of fourth graders have already tried alcohol.

For many youngsters, getting drunk is the in thing to do. While growing up, some boys and girls start to drink regularly. They drink almost anywhere. At any time.

Most kids who drink alcohol do not realize they are using a mind-changing drug. But alcohol is a drug just

like heroin or cocaine. And it has been found that those who take one kind of drug tend to use other kinds as well.

The active part of wine, beer, and all types of hard liquor is ethyl alcohol. Ethyl alcohol is produced by fermenting the sugar in corn, barley, wheat, or grapes. But fermentation can produce no more than 14 percent alcohol. At that point the fermentation stops.

The hard liquors—whiskey, gin, vodka, and brandy—are distilled drinks. Distillation is a process that increases the percentage of alcohol to between 40 and 50 percent.

One serving of a drink, no matter which kind, has about the same amount and type of alcohol. A 12-ounce can of beer, a 5-ounce glass of wine, and a 1½-

ounce shot of whiskey all contain one ounce of ethyl alcohol. Only the flavor varies.

Alcohol affects the brain most of all. It produces a feeling of pleasure, called a high. But at the same time it slows down the activity of the nerve cells, or neurons. Small amounts of alcohol produce slight changes. Larger amounts bring about greater changes.

Many young people think it's okay to have an occasional drink. They believe that a drink every once in a while will not harm them. But for many the start of heavy drinking begins just this way. The first drink leads to more drinking. Often the more a person drinks, the more he or she needs to drink.

People who must drink to feel normal suffer from a disease called alcoholism. They are dependent on, or addicted to, alcohol. About one out of every ten Americans who drink is addicted to alcohol. They are called alcoholics. Millions more drink quite heavily and may be on their way to becoming alcoholics.

A recent survey asked high school seniors about their use of alcohol. Nearly all said they had tried it, most within the month before the survey. About one third said that many of their friends got drunk at least once a week. Very few thought any harm could come from having one or two drinks a day. Almost no one believed that just trying alcohol could give you a life-long drinking problem.

Tobacco

Do you know that one million persons become first-time smokers each year? Of this number, 100,000 are children under the age of thirteen!

18

Tobacco is not exactly like the other mind-altering drugs. It does not greatly change the user's mood or behavior. Nor is there any special danger in inhaling too much tobacco smoke at once.

But, as everyone knows, it is very dangerous to smoke. Cigarette smoking is bad for your health. At best, it stains your teeth and fingers and causes coughing and breathing problems. At worst, it leads to cancer and heart disease. And it is habit-forming.

Most kids are aware of the dangers of smoking. Why, then, do so many start to smoke? Here are some reasons that they give:

"Smoking makes me feel grown-up."

"All my friends smoke."

"I don't even inhale."

"I smoke cigarettes that are low in tar and nicotine."

"I can always quit later on."

But the facts tell a different story:

The earlier you start smoking, the harder it is to quit.

The habit builds very quickly.

Smoking is more habit-forming than drinking or using most other drugs.

Almost every regular smoker is likely to get at least some of the diseases caused by cigarettes.

19

Each puff on a cigarette releases as many as 2,000 chemicals from the tobacco. By breathing in the smoke, the smokers take these chemicals into their bodies. The main ones are tar, carbon monoxide, and nicotine. All three are very harmful.

But suppose you don't inhale. Are you safe? Not really. Even without inhaling, you take in more smoke than you probably realize. Besides, tar and nicotine can be absorbed into the mouth. This is what causes such diseases as cancer of the mouth and lips.

Further, smoking creates dangers for other people. Blowing out a cloud of smoke, or even holding the cigarette without puffing, lets the chemicals enter the air. It exposes the people nearby to these chemicals just as you expose yourself.

Marijuana

Marijuana (pot or grass) is the most widely used illegal drug. The figures actually show that marijuana use among high school students is going down. But in a recent survey, one fourth of the students still said that they used the drug.

Marijuana is made from the leaves and flowers of the Indian hemp plant called *Cannabis sativa.* In its natural state it contains 40 separate chemicals. When burned, it produces more than 2,000 chemicals. Every puff brings these chemicals into the smoker's lungs and body and sends them around to every cell.

The major ingredient in marijuana is THC (tetrahydrocannabinol). THC gives users a good feeling, or high. The percentage of THC in marijuana has been increasing over the years. Ten years ago marijuana contained about 0.2 percent THC. Today it is 5 percent. And, of course, the more THC, the stronger the high.

Most Americans smoke marijuana in the form of loosely rolled cigarettes, called joints. Sometimes the marijuana is smoked in a pipe. Often smokers pass a joint or pipe from person to person, each one taking a puff.

Even one puff on a marijuana cigarette sends a good deal of THC into the body. It takes up to a week for the body to break down and excrete the THC. The exact time depends on the strength of the marijuana and the number of joints smoked. A person has to stop smoking for about a month to get rid of all the marijuana in the body.

Narcotics

Narcotics are drugs that kill pain. They include opium, morphine, heroin, and methadone. All either come from the opium poppy plant or are made in the laboratory.

Opium was one of the first narcotics people used as a painkiller. But smoking opium did more than stop pain. It also made users feel good and brought on sleep. In time people began taking opium for the high it produced and forgot its painkilling purpose.

Heroin is also called junk, smack, or horse. It gives users the biggest kick of all the narcotics. Heroin makes worries and problems seem less important. Fear and tension fade away.

Heroin is a white powder with a sharp, bitter taste. Some users sniff the powder into the nose. But more often they dissolve the powder in water that they heat in a spoon held over a match flame. Then they inject the drug into the arm.

The heroin sold on the street is almost always mixed with another material, such as sugar, starch, or powdered milk. This saves the dealer a lot of money. It also makes the heroin weaker.

Regular use of heroin is habit-forming. It also builds up a tolerance in the user for the drug. That is, the person using heroin must take larger and larger amounts of the drug to get the same result. Some people take other drugs or alcohol with the heroin. And because heroin is very expensive and the desire for the drug can be very strong, many rob and steal to pay for their habit.

Uppers and Downers

Uppers is the street name for stimulants. They speed up the heartbeat and raise the blood pressure. Users feel sharp, energetic, and alert. Caffeine is an example of a mild stimulant; cocaine is a strong one.

Caffeine is found in almost every popular beverage. Coffee, tea, cocoa, and all the cola drinks contain caffeine. Chocolate, too, has a good deal of the drug. People find that caffeine helps them be more active and think faster. It also fights feelings of tiredness and sleepiness.

Cocaine (coke or snow) is an upper that can give users a very powerful flash or rush. That is, they get short bursts of strength and good feelings. Cocaine may be breathed, or snorted, into a nostril. It can also be dissolved in water and injected directly into a muscle or

vein. Or it can be smoked in a form known as crack.

Injecting and smoking cocaine carry the greatest risks of harm. But any method can easily lead to a serious habit—and possibly death.

Amphetamines (pep pills, speed, bennies) are also stimulants. They make the user feel that there's noth-

ing he or she can't do. This high is usually soon followed by a downside crash. Users take amphetamines
by mouth or injection.

Downers are more properly known as sedatives. Another name for sedatives is depressants. In small doses
sedatives relax and calm the user; large doses put the
user to sleep.

Barbiturates and tranquilizers are two kinds of sedatives. Each can be taken by mouth or injection.

Doctors sometimes prescribe barbiturates for people
who have trouble falling asleep. They are also used to
treat high blood pressure and epilepsy. Tranquilizers
can calm the nerves, reduce pressures and stress, and
relax muscles. More powerful tranquilizers help mental
patients live more comfortable lives. The use of sedatives without a prescription can be harmful.

Hallucinogens

Hallucinogens are a particular kind of mind drug.
They change the way people see, hear, smell, or feel
objects in the world around them.

The best-known hallucinogens are LSD (acid) and
PCP (angel dust). To users taking one of these drugs,
everything seems different. Sights, sounds, and smells
may be sharper and more exciting than they actually
are.

LSD is a laboratory-made hallucinogen. The drug
looks like water. It has no color, odor, or taste. Users
swallow a drop of the liquid in a tablet or a thin square
of gelatin.

PCP is a white powder that is usually sprinkled on

leaves of parsley, mint, oregano, or marijuana. Then the leaves are rolled into a cigarette and smoked. It also may be mixed with water and taken by mouth or injected. The drug was introduced around 1967. At first it was thought to be like marijuana in its effects. That was before large numbers of PCP-caused deaths were reported. The victims had lost their lives running into speeding cars or jumping from windows after becoming very confused.

Inhalants

Glue, gasoline, spray paint, and cleaning fluid are not produced as drugs at all. But each of them gives off fumes, or vapor. And when this vapor is sniffed, or inhaled, these substances, called inhalants, become mind drugs. People inhale the fumes to get high.

The idea of sniffing glue or other inhalants just for fun is fairly new. The chemical fumes act like alcohol on the nervous system. Within seconds, the fumes produce a high. Low doses make the users act silly and giddy. Greater amounts make them even livelier and more dizzy.

Young people sometimes experiment with inhalants because they are cheap and easy to get. But the risks are great. About one out of every two longtime sniffers suffers some permanent brain damage. A few actually die by suffocation. That is because they inhale the chemical fumes with a plastic bag over their head.

How Drugs Work

All the mind drugs—legal and illegal—act on the pleasure center of the brain. Since people are all different, each individual reacts in his or her own way to a drug. For example, one person will smoke marijuana and become very happy and talkative. Someone else will smoke a joint and become quiet and withdrawn.

We know that the effects of any drug depend on five things:

1. The amount of the drug the person takes. The more of a drug someone introduces into his or her body, the more powerful the reaction.

2. The strength of the drug. Most users don't know what is in the drugs they take. The effect depends on where the drug was grown, how it was made, and how much other material was added. Some drugs also become weaker with the passage of time.

3. The way the drug is taken. Most drugs can be swallowed, smoked, injected, or inhaled. In general, swallowing takes longest and gets the least amount of the pure drug into the bloodstream and to the brain. Smoking usually gets the most drug to the brain fastest.

4. The person's body. Reactions to a drug depend on body size. In general, it takes less alcohol to make a short, thin person drunk than to make a tall, heavy person drunk. Also, the food the person has eaten may slow down or speed up the effects of some drugs.

5. The user's mood and expectations. Someone who is worried and anxious about taking a drug is more likely to have a bad experience than someone who is calm. This bad effect is sometimes called a panic reaction. On the other hand, if someone expects to get high on a drug, he or she may get that effect, even without the drug.

The Risks

Both legal and illegal drugs *can* be harmful. The effects depend on lots of factors. This makes the results hard to predict in advance.

Doctors prescribe the legal drugs to cure disease and to relieve patients of pain or discomfort. When used according to the doctor's orders, the drugs are not likely to cause problems. Trouble occurs when people take larger doses than standard. They also get into difficulties when they use the drug for purposes other than those intended.

The only drugs that are good for you are the medicines your doctor prescribes for you when you're sick. The medicine your brother or sister takes may be good for them, but not for you. Maybe it tastes good and makes them feel good. But for you, it could be very dangerous. The same, of course, is true for all the illegal drugs.

In 1971 the federal government passed the Comprehensive Drug Abuse Prevention and Control Act, or the Controlled Substances Act. This law helps to clamp down on the use of illegal drugs and the improper use

of legal drugs. It spells out penalties for the unlawful possession and sale of certain drugs.

Under the Controlled Substances Act, a first offense for unlawful possession carries up to one year's imprisonment and/or fines up to $5,000. In some cases a first offender who is under twenty-one may have the official arrest record erased after probation.

For the unlawful sale of narcotics, a first offense can get the user up to fifteen years in prison and/or fines up to $25,000. For other drugs the first offense is up to five years' imprisonment and/or fines up to $15,000.

Persons from eighteen to twenty-one who sell illegal drugs can get even more severe punishment. For a first offense the penalties are up to twice those already mentioned.

Most drug offenders are prosecuted under state laws. In some states these laws are even more severe than federal law.

.4.

Why Do Some Kids Say Yes to Drugs?

Someone asked ten-year-old Brian why he started sniffing glue. He said, "I just tried it because others were trying it. When I'd feel really bad about something, it was a way of getting to feel better. It seemed everyone I knew was taking something—sniffing glue or smoking pot. It's not only kids who are taking something to make themselves feel better. Almost everyone does."

It's a fact. Many kids—like many older people—think that it's all right for them to take something to get rid of their bad feelings. At first it may be sniffing glue. Then it could be smoking marijuana or swallowing pills. In time it might be something more dangerous, like snorting cocaine or shooting heroin. They know that it's against the law. But they say their friends have not been caught. So why should they worry?

Kids give many different reasons for saying yes to drugs. There are as many different reasons as there are different kids. But they all seem to agree on one point. They started because they wanted to change the way they felt.

By taking something, they thought, they'd feel better. Belong to a group and be accepted by others. Have more fun and be happier. Escape from pain, stress, or frustration. End boredom. Rebel against those in authority. Or just satisfy their curiosity.

Let's take a closer look at a few of these reasons.

"To Be In With the Crowd"

As you grow up, people expect more and more of you. The pressure to please others is strong. You try to fit in. It's a natural part of growing up.

The influence of your friends is especially strong during these years. To be like people of your own age is a basic need.

It's also natural to try out or experiment with new things. Wearing crazy clothes or staying out late. Doing wild dances or listening to far-out music. Or checking out drugs.

Kids may say yes to drugs so that they will be accepted by people they know. Their friends are smoking, sniffing, or drinking. And they don't want to feel left out. They are uncomfortable if they are not part of the group.

If they say no, they're afraid that others will consider them cowards or babies. Doing drugs gives them a sense of belonging. They accept dares without question.

No one likes to be called chicken or sissy for saying no to drugs. Name-calling is hard to take. No one wants others to think he or she is afraid to take some risk—is unwilling to live dangerously. Many who want to say no end up saying yes when shamed into it.

But those who hold out against drugs are not the weak ones in the group. In fact, they are the strongest members. They act as they believe they should. They don't let others force them to do what they don't want to do. They show that they are grown-up enough to make up their own minds.

The babies are those who can't resist—the ones who go along with the crowd. They are unsure of themselves. And they worry about what others say about them. Often they give in to the group—even if it means doing something that they know is wrong, stupid, or dangerous.

Can you guess the reason most kids give for starting drugs? Pressure from friends. An eleven-year-old summed it up: "My friends all wanted me to drink. And I wanted to be one of the gang."

Some fourth graders were asked how they felt about saying yes to drugs. One fourth of them said they get "some" or "a lot" of pressure to try alcohol and other drugs.

Other studies find that by sixth grade, about one child in twenty is already experimenting. In most cases, pressure is a key factor. Most young users say that they were first turned on to drugs by friends.

Almost everyone who starts using drugs does it with other people. They smoke and drink in groups. The group gives its approval. It pays special attention to the new user.

In time those who use drugs part company with those who don't. Those who are drug free avoid the

kids on drugs. Parents, teachers, and the law also line up against the drug users.

The kids who take drugs feel like outsiders. They miss their old friends. So they cling more and more to the new people—other kids who are into drugs.

Because Family Members Are Doing It

All of us are influenced by those around us. Children are especially influenced by their parents.

Kids watch—and copy—the way parents handle their feelings. They see how grown-ups fight depression and deal with stress.

Imagine Mitch's father, who has a martini every evening when he comes home from work. It is a fixed part of his day, a kind of habit. He says it gives him a chance to relax after the stress of dealing with customers all day and driving home in rush-hour traffic.

Or picture twelve-year-old Patty. She has two brothers, six and seven years old, and twin sisters, age three. Her mother says that smoking cigarettes helps her get through each day. They keep her nerves under control so that she can take care of all the kids.

Sometimes the twins are so demanding that Patty's mom gets all jumpy and upset. Then she takes a pill to calm down. She tries to take pills only when the children are not around. But Patty has seen her mother reach into the medicine chest more than once for something to make her feel better.

Many adults who use drugs give little thought to their actions. They don't realize how the things they do influence the minds and feelings of their children. Often their actions cause kids to use drugs.

The facts and figures bear this out: The majority of young smokers have parents who smoke. Teenagers who drink a lot are likely to come from homes in which heavy use of alcohol is a way of life.

The numbers of young people involved in drugs of some sort are staggering. Recently the National Institute on Drug Abuse did a countrywide survey of high school seniors. They found that:

93 percent had tried alcohol at least once.

72 percent had had alcohol in the month before the survey.

71 percent had smoked at least once.

31 percent had smoked in the month before the survey.

65 percent had used an illegal drug at least once.

Typically, someone begins to smoke if cigarettes are available at home. One or both parents consider smoking okay. Older brothers and sisters may be smoking as well. The child wants to be the same. He or she wants to find out what the others like about smoking.

In many cases drinking also begins at home. Often it is with permission from the adults who live there or visit. A young child is given a sip from someone's glass. Or, a boy or girl decides to drink the leftovers of what was prepared for grown-ups. (Usually, though, this happens without the parents' knowledge.)

Most young people start on drugs that are around. They seldom take the trouble to seek out a particular drug. This is especially true if the search involves any risk. If a certain drug can be had easily, that is the one they take.

Sometimes parents who smoke, drink, or take other drugs will try to stop their kids from doing the same. This makes some kids very angry. They distrust parents who tell children to do one thing while parents do another. The children also may become jealous of the grown-ups. Their desire to act more like adults may make some youngsters eager to try these taboo substances.

Kids who come from homes where there is drug use sometimes have a ready excuse for their drug habits. They point to their parents and say, "If they can do it, so can I." This helps them in another way, too. It makes them feel less guilty about using drugs.

"Drugs Are Fun"

Everyone likes to feel happy. The need to feel good is healthy and normal. So what's wrong with using drugs to get high? What's the matter with wanting to make yourself feel better?

The answer is simple. Bad highs, like those from drugs, may make you feel good for a while. But they harm you in the long run.

For example, in March 1987, four New Jersey teenagers killed themselves in a suicide pact. The autopsies showed that they had been taking cocaine. The experts think that they had gotten high on the drug. Then, when the effects wore off, they crashed and went into a depression. That was when they felt that life was not worth living and ended their own lives.

Our society tells us to take something for whatever ails us and everything will be fine. On radio and TV, in newspapers and magazines, on signs and billboards, we get the message: Nervous? Take a drink. Tired? Light up a cigarette. Can't sleep? Pop a pill. Why suffer? Buy something and get rid of the problem.

Don't worry about taking drugs, the ads say. All the attractive, popular, rich, successful, young people take them. Don't be a fool and miss out on the good times because of old-fashioned, fuddy-duddy ideas!

The ads are very convincing. The healthy, well-tanned sportsman looks very happy on his yacht off a lush tropical island—with a can of beer in his hand. What's wrong with that?

The well-dressed woman is driving her snazzy red sports car along a mountain road, inhaling deeply on her cigarette. What's wrong with that?

Think of ads you've seen for drinks, smokes, or pills. Ask yourself two questions: What does the ad make you think is happening? That is the fiction. And what is actually happening in this situation? That is the fact.

Here's a list for a cigarette ad prepared by a sixth grader:

FICTION	FACT
Strong, tough, and independent	Hooked and dependent on cigarettes
Attractive and appealing	Cigarettes make your breath and clothes smell bad.
Rich and successful	Cigarettes are an expensive habit. They waste a lot of money.
Strong and healthy	Cigarettes make you more apt to get sick.
Popular and loved	Most people who don't smoke dislike it when others do.

Ads usually try to give the message that drugs are a great way to make friends and have fun. The facts show the opposite. More people are not involved with drugs than take drugs. Those who say no to drugs are actually much better off than those who say yes.

To Get Back at Parents and Society

Growing up doesn't happen overnight. We all develop in stages. First we depend completely on our family. Then, after several years, we begin to feel ready to manage on our own—to test our wings, as it were.

Sooner or later we get to a stage where we rebel against our parents. If Mom says no, we say yes. If Dad says to eat less, we eat more. We fight against authority. This shows us that we are able to stand on our own two feet.

Some young people say yes to drugs as part of their rebellion. They know their parents are against drugs. By doing drugs they are striking back at their folks—and at society.

Kids sometimes feel that they're not being allowed to grow up as fast as they'd like. They say to themselves: "The more they (parents, teachers, and others) tell us not to do drugs, the more we're going to do it. We'll show them. We'll use the drugs that they've made illegal."

But those who use drugs—or think of drug-taking—should ask themselves some questions. Do drugs really make you more grown-up? Are they really a good way to get back at Mom or Dad or society? Whom do the drugs really hurt?

Rebellion is part of growing up. But not all rebellions make sense. The facts make one thing very clear. Taking drugs does not make sense. They can ruin your life and cause it to end in tragedy.

Out of Curiosity

Trying out new things teaches us much of what we know about life. We are curious. We try something new to see whether we like it or not.

Some forms of experimentation are pretty safe. Eating Japanese or Mexican food. Or trying a weird hairdo. But others, such as drinking, smoking, or doing drugs, are far more risky. That is because they can

affect your mind and body. And once you start, it can be very hard to stop.

The danger with such experiments is that the drugs can become a part of your daily life. They can also become a way of trying to solve problems.

Never taking a chance can make life very dull and boring. But it's important that the risks be reasonable. A reasonable risk means you stand to gain something if you succeed. An unreasonable risk means the opposite:

You can gain nothing.

You may lose something of value that can't be replaced.

You may harm yourself or others.

Have you thought about taking any risks lately? What about these? Which are reasonable? Which are unreasonable? Why?

1. Trying out for a school team

2. Stealing clothes from a department store

3. Jumping to the ground from a second-story window

4. Taking a very long bike ride or hiking a great distance

5. Acting in a play

6. Drinking, smoking, or taking other drugs

.5.
Why Is One Time Too Many?

After school one day, Jane suggests that you spend the afternoon at her house. Later on three other friends come over.

First you all have some soda and popcorn. Then you sit down to watch the soaps on TV. Presently Jane says, "I know where my dad keeps his joints. I'll get one. He'll never miss it. Then we can get high."

Jane goes into the next room. In a few minutes she returns. She lights the joint and starts passing it around. Each kid takes a deep drag and gives it to the next person. You're last. When Jane holds it out for you, you shake your head no.

"Oh, c'mon," she says. "You've got to try it. You don't know what you're missing. Don't listen to those creeps who tell you it's bad for you. Look at me. I've been on pot for two years. And it hasn't hurt me."

You tell her that you just don't feel like smoking. This time Jane shrugs her shoulders and gives the joint to someone else.

Although you've said no, you're confused. These are your friends. They're all nice, good kids. Would it really be so bad to try pot just one time?

Most experts give the same answer: "Yes. It is dangerous to try a drug—even once."

The reason is simple. Some people can try a drug once and never try it again. But every addict started exactly this way. One cigarette. One joint. One drink. It can mark the beginning of a lifelong habit.

Here are a few things to consider.

Can Open the Gates to Drug-Taking

Alcohol and tobacco are used more than any other drugs. What's more, they are said to open the gates to harder drugs, such as cocaine and heroin. Kids who drink or smoke are more likely to get hooked than those who steer clear of all drugs.

Time is on the side of those who say no to both

alcohol and tobacco when they're young. Those who do not drink or smoke by age twenty have a very good chance of never getting involved with drugs at all. But those who use alcohol or tobacco at an early age are at risk. They are likely to go on to other, even more dangerous, drugs.

It is hard to believe that having one drink or one cigarette can be habit-forming. Yet the facts show just that. A few drinks taken at age ten or twelve are likely to grow into a lifetime drinking problem. And if you start smoking at the same age, you have a good chance of becoming a heavy smoker.

At present about one in five teenagers smokes. Girl smokers outnumber boys who smoke.

Most kids who smoke or drink believe that they will stop someday. They know that these substances are bad for them. And they don't want to need tobacco or alcohol forever. But with each day, week, and month that goes by, it becomes harder to quit.

Cigarettes pose a special danger to kids. They introduce smoking as a way of getting a drug into the body. Once young people get used to cigarettes, some start experimenting with marijuana. Then, about one out of every three who try pot moves on to daily use. And from there it is a short step to the other illegal drugs, such as heroin, cocaine, PCP, or LSD.

You may see nothing wrong with trying a single cigarette, glass of wine, or joint. Many people feel the same way. But the facts show that plenty is wrong. Drug experimentation is never safe. It is often the beginning of a serious drug habit.

Can Cause Personal Problems

Drug users usually think that they can handle drugs better than they really can. They feel sure that they can have a safe high. They believe they will suffer no bad reactions.

Few beginning users notice the harmful effects caused by drugs. They are the last ones to see how the drug is dulling their minds. How it is destroying their bodies. How it is twisting their thoughts. How it is robbing them of happiness.

And few notice the other things that drugs do to them. Drugs make users deny the truth. Some say that they are taking less of the stuff than they really are. Or they claim to be using drugs less often than is the case. Those on drugs honestly cannot tell the way things really are.

Some people who smoke marijuana for the first time may not even get high. Since marijuana is supposed to make individuals feel good, they are disappointed. Some first-time users stop at this point. But many try again. They are looking for the high they have heard about.

Those who expect a high usually do get a good feeling from drugs. But people who are afraid of drugs may become ill. Or they may develop pot panic—a frightened feeling that makes them think they are going insane.

Tests show that drugs interfere with mental ability. Smoking marijuana, for example, makes it hard to concentrate. Studying, handling a computer, working a machine, or other tasks that need concentration become much more difficult. Sometimes a person who is high on pot forgets what happened minutes or even seconds before.

Taking drugs can interfere with school. The grades of users usually begin to drop. Students on drugs often get into trouble with teachers and principals. Some kids even have to drop out.

Drug use frequently makes it harder to get along with others. Users are jumpy and irritable. They argue more with their parents and siblings. Also, they pressure friends to start doing drugs. Trying to get friends to change their ways often leads to fights and breaks up friendships.

Of course, buying, selling, or even having an illegal drug on you is against the law. Every year thousands of drug users are caught. They all suffer shame and embarrassment. Arrests can result in a police record or even more serious consequences.

Can Be Habit-Forming

Suppose you decide to try a drug one time to see what it's like. And suppose nothing bad happens. You like its calming effect. It makes you forget your troubles. And it carries you off to a make-believe world.

Very soon your body and brain send out the message: "Let's try this again! This is fun!"

In the beginning the message isn't too strong or powerful. So you just wait for a chance to take the drug again. Each time it comes along, you grab it. You want to get the same good feelings another time.

With each use, the message gets stronger: "Hey, this feels good! I need more of the drug."

By now you don't wait for someone to offer you the drug. You go looking for it. And the message is louder and more demanding. It says, "I've got to have the drug! Get me more!"

At this point you have a drug habit. You are dependent on the drug. You have become a drug addict.

Experts find that most children say no a number of times before they say yes for the first time. Sometimes

the pressure gets too great. Other times they just become too curious.

Starting drugs isn't always fun. Many kids don't like the taste of alcohol at first. Cigarettes make them cough and cause their eyes to water. They may get no charge from their first joint. And many get badly frightened or become sick when they start with the other drugs.

"Don't worry," they're told, "it'll get better." And it usually does. Those who keep trying drugs usually find one that they like.

Many users get fooled by drugs. At first they can take them or leave them alone. So they think this will always be true. But as they get deeper into drugs, they find that they need them more and more. They go on to more frequent use—with friends, at parties—and then alone. They no longer wait for others to offer them drugs. They seek out drugs on their own.

Drugs cost money. So many children look for the cheapest ones to take. They sniff glue or gasoline. They smoke cigarettes or drink cheap wine or whiskey. Some buy crack, a less expensive and more deadly form of cocaine.

As their bodies get used to the drugs, they long for stronger stuff. Many get desperate. They get money any way they can to pay for the drugs. If they feel guilty about robbing or stealing, they escape by stepping up their drug use.

You've read how now-and-then use can lead to regular use. Regular users have drugs on their minds much of the time. They spend a lot of time planning the next high. Many are still able to keep up with normal life activities at this stage, but it's not easy.

Addiction, or dependency, is the last stage. It occurs when people feel they need drugs so much that they can't live without them. Dependent users think only about drugs. Everything they do has but one purpose: to get high. Without drugs they suffer extreme mental or physical pain. They are willing to do anything to get the next fix. The drugs become a crutch to get them through each day.

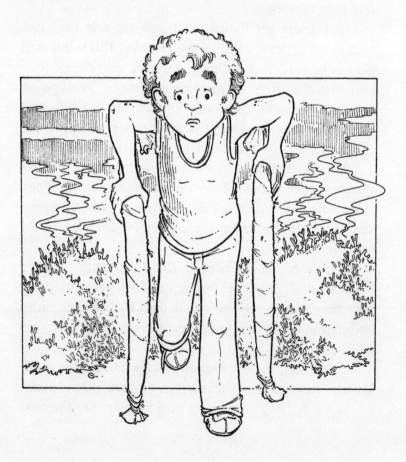

Drugs completely take over the lives of addicts. Sometimes they realize that they are being destroyed by their drug habit. So they try to break free. But breaking a drug habit at this late stage is hard. It can be a very long and painful process.

Can Even Kill You

"Drinking makes me feel happy and helps me have a good time," wrote one thirteen-year-old in his diary. These were practically his last words. Shortly afterward, while crossing a street, he was killed by a car. The police reported that he had been drinking. Witnesses said the boy had staggered into traffic without looking out for cars.

Nearly 8,000 youngsters are killed each year in accidents involving alcohol. Another 40,000 are seriously injured. Some of these victims, though, did not have one drop to drink. They were killed or hurt by others who had been drinking.

Alcohol can kill in another way. If you drink a lot of alcohol—say a pint of whiskey at one time—it can cause your death. The alcohol interferes with the part of your brain that controls breathing. You stop breathing and you die.

Smoking cigarettes has been called slow-motion suicide. A pint of whiskey can kill you in a matter of minutes. Smoking can take your life over a number of years. Five, ten, twenty years after you start smoking, your doctor may notice little spots of cancer on your lungs. Or you may cough and wheeze so much that you can't catch your breath. Or you may suffer a fatal heart attack.

As for marijuana, even a one-time high can get you into big trouble. Smoking pot makes some people reckless and careless. You can become overly sure of yourself and take foolish risks. Some people are hurt or killed while high on marijuana.

Twelve-year-old Terry was very proud that he was chosen to play on the high school softball team at the Fourth of July picnic. He was especially happy when his teammates invited him to join them for a victory celebration after the game. At first everyone was drinking beer. Terry refused, saying that he just didn't like the taste. Then they began passing joints around. Terry was too embarrassed to say no again. So he took a big, deep drag on the joint each time it was handed to him.

After smoking, the fellows started shooting off firecrackers. Someone suggested a game. They would see who could hold a lit firecracker longest before it exploded. Although Terry was feeling dizzy from the marijuana, he decided to play.

A friend handed Terry a firecracker and lit the string fuse. Terry wanted everyone to see how brave he was. So he tried to hold it a long while. But he waited a bit too long. The firecracker exploded in his hand. Terry never fully recovered from his injuries.

Too much of a drug can be disastrous. Children, for example, can be made sick or even be killed by smaller amounts of a drug than adults. Young people are usually lighter than grown-ups. And the less you weigh, the more powerful the effect of a drug. The same amount of a drug that gets a 165-pound man high can kill a 90-pound boy.

Also, many drugs sold on the street are not pure. The drug dealers add cheap filler to make their supplies go further and increase their profit. The additives are sometimes dangerous chemicals. Taken with the drug itself, they may make the user very sick or even kill him or her.

Some drug users are eager for an even better high. So they take various drugs at the same time. Combining drugs is very common—and extremely dangerous. Certain mixtures of drugs can kill. A well-known example is alcohol and sleeping pills. For some people, this mix stops normal breathing and results in death.

.6.
How Can You Say No to a Friend?

Kids worry a lot about having friends. Most everyone wants to be popular and belong to a group. To fit in and be accepted by others is a common ambition.

Few things feel as good as having friends. When asked what friends do for them, this is what several kids said:

FRED (11):   "Friends help me feel less lonely."

SAMMY (12): "Friends make me feel safe."

MARIA (10): "Friends make me feel equal to someone."

SUSAN (10): "Friends give me someone to trust."

Most young people try to be like their friends, like the group. There's nothing wrong with that. The problem comes in when you feel you have to accept all of your friends' beliefs for them to like you.

Being friends with someone means finding ways to get along. Sometimes you give in a little. Sometimes your friend is the one to give in.

But what happens when your friend pressures you to do something that you don't want to do? Perhaps to try a drug that you don't want. Do you give in to your friend? Or do you stand up for your beliefs?

Growing up means making your own choices. It means deciding when you want to go along with someone else and when you want to do your own thing. It means choosing what you believe is right for you, even if it's different from what others have chosen.

When you know something is wrong, you have to say no. Even to a friend, and even if it means losing that person's friendship.

Lots of kids have ways to resist the pressure to go along. Have you? Perhaps these examples will suggest ways to withstand the influence of friends who take drugs.

Believe in Yourself

Sally was in the locker room getting into her gym shorts. Anne was next to her. After looking around to see that no one else was nearby, Anne started speaking softly to Sally. "Ruth's parents are going to be away tonight. She's invited a few of us over. Her boyfriend is coming, too. He's bringing a bottle of gin. Want to come?"

Sally stared at Anne for a second before saying anything. "I'd really like to come. I like you and I like Ruth. But I don't drink. So I can't come. But thanks for asking me."

"We're not drunks or drug addicts," Anne replied. "We just like to drink every once in a while. It relaxes everyone and we all have a better time. Come on, say yes."

"I think it's wrong to drink," Sally answered more firmly. "It's bad for you and it goes against my beliefs. Sorry, I can't come. Maybe next time, if there's no drinking."

"You know," Anne whispered to Sally, "I feel the way you do. I really don't like drinking either. I hate to see the other kids get drunk and then get sick and throw up. But I just don't know how to say no. I wish I could stick to my guns the way you do."

Sally felt good that she was strong enough to stand up for what she held true. She didn't go along with the others just to be their friend. As a result, Anne respected her more, not less. And Sally kept her feelings of self-worth.

It is easier to say no if you realize that you are special—a one-of-a-kind human being. Remember—there never has been anyone else like you—and there never will be!

Keep in mind that you are a thinking person. Able to tell right from wrong. Able to figure things out and act reasonably. And able to become the very best that you can be.

As long as you have respect for yourself, you'll be able to say no to drugs. If you feel good about yourself, you won't risk ruining your life. As Buddy, age twelve, says, "I don't drink or smoke because that's just not me."

Talk Your Way Out of the Situation

Tom came home one afternoon and found his big brother George and some of George's friends smoking pot.

"Here," George said to Tom with a smile. "Have a puff." He held out the joint.

"No, thanks," Tom said.

"Don't you want to hang out with us?" George asked.

"Yeah. But I don't want to smoke."

Tom turned to George's friends. "Hey, did you watch the play-offs on TV last night? I thought what happened in the last few minutes was terrific, didn't you?"

In a minute everyone was talking about the game. By changing the subject, Tom was able to refuse the drug and still be part of the group.

Saying no to drugs in a firm and definite way usually does the trick. If you say it like you really mean it, the message gets through most of the time. If not, you can keep on talking.

Perhaps you can come up with a suggestion for something else to do:

FRIEND: "How about a pot party tonight?"

YOU: "No. But would you like to come bowling with me instead?"

Sometimes the best approach is to answer with a joke:

FRIEND: "Psst. Are you into booze?"

YOU: "No, but there's a whole can of Coca-Cola inside me."

FRIEND: "Do you want to get high on crack?"

YOU: "When I want to get high, I use a ladder."

FRIEND: "How about a joint?"

YOU: "What do you have in mind—an elbow, wrist, or knee?"

Sometimes saying no takes practice. Practice makes perfect. Try out your answers in front of a mirror. This may make it easier in real life.

Consider these situations in which people might be trying to push drugs on you. Pretend that you're there. How would you react to each one? Think of as many different ways of saying no as possible:

An older kid whom you like and trust asks you to buy drugs for her.

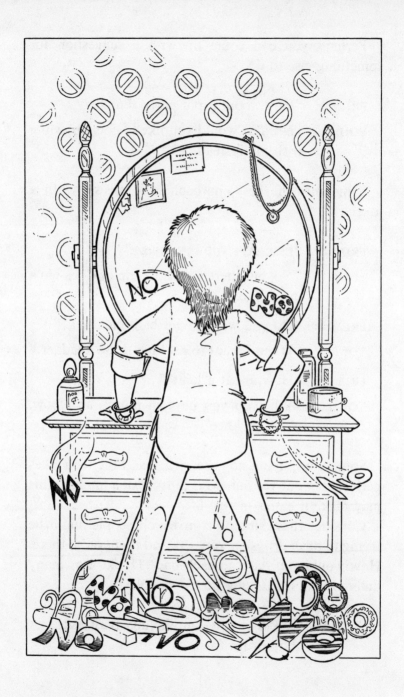

Someone in your class calls you a baby because you won't sniff glue.

A few kids in school have a club that you would like to join. But they tell you that they sometimes smoke crack afterward.

Someone approaches you outside school and offers you free drugs.

You're at the ball park and someone offers you a beer.

A neighbor promises you money if you will deliver drugs for him.

Take Yourself Out of the Situation

Every Friday evening Sara and a bunch of kids from her school go to a downtown movie. After the show, they all head for the pizza parlor, where everyone has a slice.

One night Sara spotted some girls she wanted to know better. They were sitting at a big round table in the back of the restaurant.

"Hi," Sara said as she pulled up a chair and joined them. The girls were nice and included her in their conversation. Sara felt good until someone took out a pack of cigarettes. Everyone lit up. Only Sara refused.

"What are you afraid of?" said one girl. "It's only a cigarette."

"Yeah," chimed in another, "are you too goody-goody to smoke?"

Some of the others laughed. Sara thought of lots of things she could say. But she decided not to say anything. Instead she looked around the restaurant.

"Oops, there's someone I have to see," she said, getting up. "See ya."

Drugs often pop up where and when you least expect them—your own home, a friend's house, or at school. These are among the most likely places.

Often the best thing to do is to get out of the situation. Just pick up and leave. Go to the next table. Move into the next room. Call home if you need to. Ask someone for a ride.

If you're in a group that's not right for you, find another one. Decide where you would rather be; then go there.

Avoid Friends Who Take Drugs

Larry always wanted to be friends with Bert. Bert was very popular. He was class president; all the girls were in love with him. He was a good athlete and had a great sense of humor.

Larry was the quiet, shy type. Very smart, he got straight A's in school and read many books the other kids had never even heard of. Even though he had lots of friends, he really wanted to be liked by Bert.

One day Bert invited Larry to try out the basketball net his father had set up behind his house. Larry was thrilled.

As they walked home, Bert pulled a crumpled joint out of his jacket pocket. "Let's smoke," he urged. "It'll get rid of the stress of school."

"No, thanks, I don't need drugs to relax," Larry replied.

"You should try it," Bert insisted. "Everyone smokes."

Larry still refused. But from then on, Larry kept away from Bert. Larry knew that kids who use drugs tend to press drugs on their friends. He wanted to keep away from danger. Being Bert's friend was not such a good idea after all, he decided.

Sometimes it helps to think of kids who use drugs as quicksand—something that can swallow you up if you get too close.

Would you knowingly walk into quicksand? Probably not. You'd keep away from it. Well, friends who use drugs are at least as dangerous. So are the places where people often use drugs.

You can say no to drugs by hanging out with friends who don't use them. Spend your time with people who have beliefs and values like your own. Try to find kids with similar interests. Being with people who are like you may save you from the pressure to do things you don't want to do.

Think about having more than one or two friends. Few friends, if they're busy or not around, can make you feel pretty lonely. Larger groups make it easier to resist peer pressure.

Parents sometimes say that belonging to a group is a bad thing. The reason? Some kids seem to go along with the crowd in everything. The way they look. Where they go. And their experiments with drugs.

That's why it's important to pick your groups carefully. Avoid ones that make you uneasy and uncomfortable. And don't go back to friends who try to force you to do things that you know are wrong.

Experts find that kids who break the rules look for others like themselves. For instance, kids who smoke

cigarettes or drink beer usually need friends to urge them on.

Some kids are able to turn away from things they don't approve of. Others can't. One fifth grader says, "I have some friends who push me to do things I don't think are right. I don't really want to do these things. But if I'm going to be friends with them, what can I do?"

What suggestions would you offer?

Talk to Someone You Trust

Peggy was walking to school. She passed a teenage boy sitting on a bench.

"Hey, want to get high?" the fellow asked.

Peggy shook her head no. But he got up and followed her. "This is good stuff," he insisted, moving very close to her.

Her heart was beating hard, but she didn't say anything. She just kept walking. After a while, the boy turned away. Peggy ran the rest of the way to school, shaking with fright.

When she got to class, she told her teacher what had happened. Her teacher let her talk out the whole experience. This calmed Peggy down. Her teacher's interest and concern helped Peggy decide what she could do if the same thing ever happened again.

It usually helps to open up and tell someone about a drug offer. Sharing your feelings with someone you know and trust restores your faith in others. Especially if you feel unsure about drugs.

Just knowing that you don't have to face a problem

alone makes all the difference. It also helps to listen to others who have been in similar situations. Learn how they worked things out, what they know about drugs, how they avoided running with the crowd.

Parents are usually the first people kids turn to. If that is hard for you, try your teacher, school psychologist, or some other adult who cares. Sometimes all you need is a close friend who doesn't use drugs.

Keep in mind that most people know that taking drugs is dangerous. They may not approve of drug use. But they respect people who are honest and open about drug problems.

Try to Help a Friend Who Takes Drugs to Quit

Melissa was feeling low. She had just failed a big math test. And to make matters worse, her dog had run away from home.

That evening Melissa's parents went out. A friend was coming over to cheer her up and do homework together.

"Here, have one of my mother's pills," her friend said when she saw how sad Melissa felt. "I sometimes take them. They'll make you feel good."

Melissa knew that pills weren't good to take unless they were prescribed for you. Otherwise, they could really do harm.

"No, thanks," she said. "I just know popping pills won't bring my puppy back. And if I get started on pills, I'm afraid something much worse may happen."

Melissa turned on the tape recorder. The music was loud and had a terrific beat. "Let's dance instead," Melissa urged. "Dancing helps me get out of a bad mood faster than anything."

Peer pressure works two ways. Others can try to get you to take drugs. But you can also try to help others quit drugs. By saying no—and explaining why—you might get others to think twice about smoking, drinking, or taking drugs of any kind.

Suppose you have a friend who is good in sports but also likes to smoke and drink. You might point out how drugs slow people down and interfere with reflexes.

To play well you need fast reactions. These depend on a body in perfect working order. The eyes need to see clearly. The brain has to handle the information quickly. The nerves must be able to carry the message immediately. And the muscles should respond instantly. Otherwise, the game or race is lost.

Someday someone may thank you for helping him or her stop drugs.

Learn to Deal With Rejection

Joan and Ellen had been best friends since they were seven years old. When they were in fifth grade, Ellen's family moved to a bigger house on the other side of town. The girls still spoke on the phone and saw each other every few weeks.

Recently Ellen had begun acting very cold to Joan. She broke dates and ignored her if other people were around.

When they were together, Ellen spoke mostly about her new friends. She raved about their parties and told

how much fun they had. She gave Joan all the details on the first time she tried pot and told her about experiments with cocaine.

Joan noticed that Ellen seemed nervous and on edge when they were together. Ellen lost her temper and cursed when little things went wrong. She blew up if Joan said anything she disagreed with. Especially if Joan said something against drugs. "Oh, grow up. Everybody is into drugs today!" she once shouted.

Before too long Ellen stopped phoning Joan. Ellen found many excuses for not getting together. Within a year the friendship was over.

Losing friends as a result of drugs can make you feel rotten. But it's important to understand why. Once you do, it is easier to handle the bad feelings.

Drugs change people. They change the way they feel and the way they behave. Beginning drug users may become easily annoyed or angered, especially by little things. Often they don't stop to consider what they say or do.

Feelings of guilt are common, too. Kids start taking drugs as a way of getting rid of bad feelings. The drug makes them feel good. But whatever caused the bad feelings has not gone away. They may blame themselves for feeling good in spite of the bad things that are going on. And using illegal drugs can make them worry about getting caught.

Seeing you walk away from drugs may make them uncomfortable. Inside, they don't like what they're doing. That's why they either try to get you to join them or they break up the friendship.

Once you understand why friends on drugs may turn away from you, you can deal with the rejection. You will not let it lower your self-image.

Abraham Lincoln knew how important it is to be true to yourself. He said: "If at the end . . . I have lost every other friend on earth, I shall at least have one friend left, and that friend shall be down inside me."

.7.

How Can You Say No After You've Said Yes?

Suppose you're a kid who has already said yes to drugs.

Do you know that tobacco

- makes you nervous and jittery?
- harms your lungs and heart?
- can kill you with cancer or heart disease?

Do you know that alcohol

- affects the way your brain works?
- slows your reaction time?
- interferes with your coordination and body movements?

Do you know that marijuana

- dulls the mind?
- damages the memory?
- speeds up the heart?

Do you know that other drugs

- can cause serious physical and mental reactions?

- can destroy friendships and career plans?
- can lead to crime?
- can make you depend on them forever?

Just knowing these facts may make you decide to stop smoking, drinking, or using other drugs. Or are you afraid it's too late because you already have the habit?

Sometimes it's not so easy to stop drugs. But there's an old Chinese proverb that says "A journey of 1,000 miles starts with a single step." If you want to be free of drugs, you have to take the first step.

Get in Touch with Your Good Feelings

Imagine these situations:

Your good friend from out of town is coming to visit. You feel a rush of excitement and energy.

You've won a gold medal in the school Olympics. You feel proud and have a sense of accomplishment.

You've aced an exam. You feel like jumping for joy.

You've been given two tickets for a World Series game. You're so happy that you're afraid you'll burst.

You see a really funny show on TV. You laugh so hard tears run down your cheeks.

Has anything like this happened to you? If so, then you know what it's like to feel really good.

Athletes get real highs from scoring goals or runs. Students get kicks from solving problems or getting A's. Pianists get turned on by mastering hard pieces and playing them in public. Painters are excited by the colors and shapes in a work of art they are creating.

Feeling good, scientists tell us, is mostly chemical. When you're doing something you enjoy and are getting satisfaction, your brain produces extra amounts of certain natural chemicals. These chemicals are called endorphins.

Endorphins give you a natural high. They have the same effect on the mind as certain illegal drugs. The endorphins block any feeling of pain. They pick up your mood. Make you feel more relaxed. Give you a feeling of well-being. Thanks to the endorphins, everything seems brighter and better.

The natural highs are like drug highs in many ways. But they're better. They do not harm your body or mind. You can't overdose on them. They won't lead to addiction. And they're not illegal.

Almost any fun activity brings about changes in your body. Your heart rate and blood flow speed up. Your blood pressure rises. Your arteries grow wider, especially the ones supplying blood to the muscles you're using. And your brain produces more endorphins.

Of course, not every moment is a high. And not every high is immediate. But overall, doing things you enjoy gives you extra-special good feelings.

Think of all the different things you can do to get these feelings. The physical things—jogging, swimming, biking, hiking. The mental things—reading a great mystery, playing chess, working with a computer, learning a magic trick, mastering a new language. The social things—joining a club, being part of a team, going on a camping trip, going to the movies with a friend. The artistic things—writing a poem, fooling around on the piano, painting in watercolors, dancing freestyle to music. The everyday special things—cooking dinner for the family, doing home repairs, growing plants, raising animals.

When you feel down and think of taking something, do something instead. Throw yourself into it. You'll be amazed at how great you'll feel. And you can get this same high over and over again.

Get Rid of Bad Feelings
You may have turned to drugs because of bad feelings. Things may have happened that made you scared, angry, disappointed, or bored.

The drugs may mask the bad feelings for a while. But when the drug wears off, you find that you're no better off than before. In fact, things are probably worse now.

Most kids get rid of bad feelings without drugs. So can you. Here are a few ways others deal with sadness and gloom without drugs.

Billy has a problem. He gets frightened every time he has to speak in public. He shakes if he has to give a report in class. His mouth gets dry. Sometimes he even gets tongue-tied. What can he—or you—do about feeling afraid?

Sometimes, we said, it helps to talk about scared feelings with someone. But what else can you do?

Usually it helps to go ahead and try the thing that scares you. Many times this drives your scared or shy feelings away. Billy forces himself to speak in front of others. He reports that it is getting easier to talk to a group.

Once you find the courage to do what you fear doing, you will feel better. You may even feel proud and surprised at how well things turn out. And each time you will be less afraid than the time before.

Of course, there are times when you really should be scared. Like when someone dares you to do something harmful or dangerous. Then being afraid can save you from hurting yourself or someone else.

Look at this situation. Susie is very angry with her older sister, Julie. Every time Julie's friends are around, the same thing happens. Julie bosses her and makes her run errands. Susie gets so mad that she usually storms out of the house, slamming the door as hard as she can. Inside herself she feels angry and helpless.

All of us feel angry when we think we have been treated unfairly. Or we get mad when we think we are being left out of things. At times it can be hard to get over our angry feelings.

What can Susie do about her feelings? And what can you do about such feelings?

You might try talking things over instead of slamming doors. Susie sometimes tells Julie why she is angry. That helps. She also talks with the rest of her family. They give her some ideas on how to deal with her sister's bossiness.

Talking over your angry feelings is better than keeping them locked up inside you. It is surely better than taking something to cover up the feelings. As long as the angry feelings are inside, you will feel upset and unhappy.

Another way is to try to think of what you may be doing to cause the bad feelings. Susie now tries to make sure that she is not annoying Julie. Maybe Julie needs more time by herself. Or she wants to be alone with her friends—without Susie being around.

Also, be sure that you are not misunderstanding the other person's words and actions. Could Julie be trying to make Susie feel useful by giving her things to do?

Some kids work off angry feelings by writing about them. If you think someone has treated you unfairly, you might write an angry letter. Tell how you feel and why. Writing the letter often gets rid of the angry feelings. Later, though, you may want to throw the letter away.

Suppose there's nobody around to talk with. And you don't feel like writing a letter. What then?

Do something else for a while. Doing other things can help calm you down until you have a chance to talk about your feelings.

Try Something New

Most of us do the same sorts of things—day after day. We get into habits or ruts. But everyone can find something new that he or she would really like to do. What would be your first choice?

Many kids are turned on by music. It may be the beat of the latest hit song or the beautiful melody of an old folk song. Perhaps it's the excitement of Dixieland jazz or the stirring sounds of a symphony orchestra.

Making music can also give pleasure. You can learn to play an instrument and either play by yourself or join a band or orchestra. Or you can sing in a chorus.

Find out for yourself how music improves your mood and boosts your energy. Feel how it triggers strong emotions and opens the door to your imagination. As someone once said, "It's hard to feel down when the volume is up!"

If music isn't your thing, find something else to try. Do you enjoy painting or drawing? What about creating a masterpiece for your room?

Can you express yourself in writing? Don't wait for a class assignment. Keep a diary or start a book of poetry. Set your thoughts down on paper. This may help you get in touch with your feelings and release ones that are bottled up.

How about dancing? It can be jazz, tap, disco, ballet, ballroom, or folk. Or you can make up your own dances to go with any music you like. Dance is a terrific way of expressing yourself. Some people find that they can just dance their troubles away. And it is also a good way to make contact with others.

Have you ever tried acting? Join a theater group at

a community center or in school and see whether working onstage is for you.

Do you have a camera? Try telling a story with photographs. Maybe take pictures that capture the spirit of the time of year.

Does making money get your juices flowing? Some of the richest men and women in the country started their own businesses when very young. Delivering newspapers or grocery orders is one way to start. Also, mowing lawns, shoveling snow, and baby-sitting. You can even start out selling pens in school or boxes of cookies in the neighborhood.

Think of hobbies. Would you like to try

- playing chess or checkers?
- collecting stamps or coins?
- working with a computer?
- caring for pets?
- writing to a pen pal?

It doesn't matter what you do. Just getting absorbed in something can make you feel wonderful. It can make you feel proud of your accomplishment. It can raise your self-concept.

So try something new. Just do it. Feel good about it. Get high on it!

Seek Professional Help

We all need other people with whom we can talk over our problems. Especially if the problems are about feelings that have been buried for a long time. Uncovering these sore spots is not easy. It can take a lot of courage to begin. And much time to continue. But the rewards can be great and long-lasting.

Putting your thoughts into words makes things clearer to you. And it gives others a chance to find out what is going on in your mind. They react to what you are saying. That can help you feel less alone.

Friends and family are usually the first ones we turn to when we have problems. But they may not always be able to help. That is when it may be a good idea to speak with an expert. The experts include your family doctor; the school psychologist; your minister, priest, or rabbi; or anyone trained as a drug counselor.

When you meet with a counselor, a psychiatrist, a social worker, or other helping professional, you can feel free to talk about everything and anything. Drugs, lies, feelings of anger, thoughts of suicide—these are just a few things you can discuss. All that you say is treated as a secret. It is strictly confidential. Nothing will get back to parents, teachers, or the police. This kind of help is based on trust: You trust the therapist not to repeat anything you say; he or she trusts you to be as honest as possible.

How do you know when it's time to call on a professional? This list of questions can help you decide. If you answer yes to some or all of them, you should think about going for help.

Have I lost interest in things I used to enjoy?

Do I have trouble keeping my mind on schoolwork?

Do I cry a lot?

Am I sad and depressed much of the time?

Do I spend a lot of my time sleeping?

Have I lost my appetite?

Am I often angry and irritable?

Do I sometimes think about suicide?

Do I feel that I have nothing to live for?

Have I started doing drugs to make myself feel good?

For example, Lisa had trouble making friends. When someone asked her to join a group, she accepted right away. It was like magic. She felt that she belonged and that they really cared for her.

But soon Lisa found out things about her new friends that she didn't like. They were into drugs. They did not always tell her the truth about pills and stuff they had talked her into taking. She had some bad trips. And she was scared at the way her personality was changing.

Lisa made up her mind to speak to the school psychologist. He listened to Lisa's story. Among other things, he gave her accurate information about drugs—their effects, risks, and so on.

Based on the facts, Lisa decided to get out of the gang. She stopped taking drugs. The psychologist suggested a one-day-at-a-time approach. Each day Lisa planned things to do with her time. She tried out for a part in the school play. Rehearsals kept her busy every afternoon and some evenings. Lisa loved being part of the cast.

Gradually Lisa began making friends. She felt better

about herself. It was good being in charge of her life for a change. In fact, her new feelings about herself made her more open to others. Her phone rang more, and kids were knocking at her door.

Lisa also joined the local Just Say No Club. There are about 15,000 of them in schools, community centers, and Y's across the country. They're groups of young people who help each other avoid starting drugs. And they help those who are trying to stop.

Of course, not all kids can stop drugs as easily as Lisa. Those who have been on drugs for a long time need special help. They may have to go to a drug therapist, a therapeutic community, or a treatment center. Often they find names and addresses of such places in the telephone book.

A drug therapist usually sees the person once or twice a week. The therapist and drug user talk about many things—everything from how the person started drugs to how to stop taking them.

Therapeutic communities are places drug users can go for help. Some are residential, where a number of people who were on drugs live together. They help one another break free of the habit.

Most treatment centers are part of hospitals. Such centers use a variety of talking therapies plus medical care to help former drug users. It can take a long time to break a strong drug habit.

But breaking a drug habit is not enough. It must go along with building a new life. This includes many things: Finding new values and skills. Discovering new ways of handling feelings. Thinking less about yourself and more about others. Putting an end to the lies and

denial that are part of drug behavior. Breaking up friendships with people on drugs and making new friends.

Perhaps you've made up your mind to say no—even though you've said yes. Then you may want to make this promise to yourself. It is the same pledge many kids have already taken:

I agree

- not to drink alcohol.
- not to smoke cigarettes.
- not to do any other drugs.
- and, above all, not to make any exceptions.

When is the best time to make this pledge to yourself?

The best time is right now!

Understand Some Terms

acid   slang for LSD

addiction   a habit in which the user cannot stop taking drugs

alcohol   a drug found in wine, beer, and hard liquor

alcoholism   a dependency on alcohol

amphetamines   drugs that speed up the nervous system

angel dust   slang for PCP

barbiturates   drugs that act as sedatives

bennies   slang for amphetamines

cocaine   a drug that comes from coca leaves

coke   slang for cocaine

crack   a very dangerous form of cocaine that is smoked

depressants   another name for sedatives

downers   slang for sedatives

flash   a sudden feeling of pleasure

hallucinogens   drugs that make people see, hear, or smell things that are not really there

heroin   a narcotic produced from morphine

high   a feeling of pleasure

horse slang for heroin

inhalants substances that give off fumes or vapors; when breathed in, they make users high

joint slang for marijuana cigarette

junk slang for heroin

LSD lysergic acid diethylamide, a hallucinogen that is made in the laboratory

marijuana a drug made from the leaves and flowers of the cannabis plant

narcotics pain-killing drugs such as opium, morphine, heroin, and methadone that are made from the poppy flower or produced in laboratories

opium a drug that comes from the opium poppy plant

PCP phencyclidine, a hallucinogen

pep pills slang for amphetamines

reefer slang for marijuana cigarette

rush a short burst of strength and good feelings

sedatives drugs that calm or put a person to sleep

smack slang for heroin

snow slang for cocaine

speed slang for amphetamines

stimulants drugs that speed up the heartbeat and raise the blood pressure in users

THC tetrahydrocannabinol, the main ingredient in marijuana

tobacco a leaf that contains a number of drugs that pass into the body when smoked

tranquilizers drugs that make users feel calm and relaxed

trip slang for a drug experience

uppers drugs, such as amphetamines, that speed up the nervous system

Further Reading

Berger, Gilda. *Addiction: Its Causes, Problems, and Treatment.* New York: Franklin Watts, 1982.

————. *Crack: The New Drug Epidemic.* New York: Franklin Watts, 1987.

————. *Drug-Testing: A New Weapon to Fight the Drug Crisis.* New York: Franklin Watts, 1987.

————. *Smoking Not Allowed: The Debate.* New York: Franklin Watts, 1987.

Hyde, Margaret O., and Bruce G. Hyde. *Know About Drugs.* New York: McGraw-Hill, 1979.

Madison, Arnold. *Drugs and You.* New York: Julian Messner, 1982.

Seixas, Judith. *Alcohol: What It Is, What It Does.* New York: Greenwillow, 1977.

————. *Pot: What It Is, What It Does.* New York: Greenwillow, 1979.

————. *Tobacco: What It Is, What It Does.* New York: Greenwillow, 1981.

Sonnett, Sherry. *Smoking.* New York: Franklin Watts, 1977.

Woods, Geraldine, and Harold Woods. *Cocaine.* New York: Franklin Watts, 1985.

About the Author

GILDA BERGER is the author of many other informative books for young people, most recently *Drug-Testing: A New Weapon to Fight the Drug Crisis* and *Crack: The New Drug Epidemic*, published by Franklin Watts. She felt a need to write a book that would suggest to the reader "how to take control of one's own life, how to obtain support from family, how to find drug-free friends and professional resources within the community, and how to fill the day with satisfying, rewarding things to do."

Ms. Berger lives in Great Neck, New York, with her husband Melvin, also a writer.

About the Illustrator

TED ENIK's humorous illustrations have appeared in a number of books, including *Encyclopedia Brown's Book of Wacky Crimes* by Donald J. Sobol. Mr. Enik lives in New York City.